Little Passports®
A GLOBAL ADVENTURE

The Shadow
Snake Chase

Written by Megan E. Bryant

Illustrated by Carrie English

Sam & Sofia's Scooter Stories

First paperback edition printed in 2020 by Little Passports, Inc.
Copyright © 2020 Little Passports
All rights reserved
Manufactured in China
10 9 8 7 6 5 4 3 2 1

Little Passports, Inc.
27 Maiden Lane, Floor 4, San Francisco, CA 94108
www.littlepassports.com
ISBN: 978-1-953148-05-6

Contents

1

The Secret Staircase

As Sam approached the bright green door at the end of the hall, the first thing he noticed was the way it gleamed from a fresh coat of paint. Even the doorknob and the brand-new hinges seemed to sparkle. When Sam tried to turn the doorknob, though, it didn't budge. He frowned, then read the note from his best friend, Sofia, again.

Hi Sam!

Come to the last door in the hallway behind the gym. You're going to LOVE it.

P.S. — The doorknob sticks. Give it a wiggle.

-Sofia

Well, Sam thought, *at least I know I found the right door.*

He tapped and twisted the doorknob, but it was still jammed. He even braced himself against the wall to pull. Nothing! Just as he was about to give up, he stepped back and gave the knob a gentle wiggle, and the door swung open.

Thank goodness for Sofia's note. Sam stepped through the door to find a steep and narrow staircase leading up to another door. How many secret doors were there?! Just when he thought he'd explored every inch of Compass Community Center, he found out there was even more to discover!

His heart thundering with anticipation, Sam climbed the stairs two at a time. The second door was easier to open than the first. Sam walked through it and found himself blinking in the brightness of full sunshine. It took him a moment to realize where he was: a rooftop deck!

"You made it!" Sofia's voice carried over to him as Sam stepped out onto the deck.

"I—this—whoa!" Sam stammered as he marveled at the space.

"Isn't it amazing up here?" Sofia said, throwing her arms out wide. "I feel like a bird! Look, you can see almost all of Compass Court!"

Sam cupped his hand over his eyes to shield them from the sun so he could get a better view.

Over the guardrail, he could see the house where Sofia lived with her parents, Mama Lyla and Papai Luiz. Across the way was the house where he lived with Aunt Charlie. From here, Sam could even see his front door, where he had found the note from Sofia.

Sam lifted his camera to his face.

Click-click! Click-click!

Sofia was right: This bird's-eye view of Compass Court was incredible.

"Hi, Sam," Mama Lyla, called from across the deck. She was arranging some lounge chairs

with Sofia's dad, Luiz. "What do you think of our deck? We just finished the renovations yesterday."

"I love it!" Sam replied.

"We were pretty worried last week that it wouldn't be finished in time," Papai Luiz said. "But everything worked out just right."

"Finished in time for what?" Sam asked.

"It's a big surprise, and they haven't told me, either," Sofia said. "Believe me, I've asked."

"You really want to know?" a new voice asked.

"Aunt Charlie!" Sofia said, turning around.

Sam's aunt Charlie stood in the doorway, carrying two big boxes.

"I should've known you had something to do with all this," Sam teased his aunt.

"Sorry to keep you guessing," Aunt Charlie said, wiggling her eyebrows as Sam and Sofia hurried forward to help with the boxes. "We decided to wait to tell you until everything was ready."

Mama Lyla started spreading out some pillows and picnic blankets. "Our friends and neighbors from the Compass Court Science Club are coming up later tonight."

"We're all going to *gaze* at something together," Papai Luiz added.

"The view of Compass Court?" Sam asked.

"Think bigger . . . and farther . . ." Aunt Charlie said, " . . . and up!" She swept her arm toward the clouds.

"The sky!" Sam and Sofia said together.

"You got it," Aunt Charlie said.

"Tonight," said Papai Luiz, "will be the first-ever Compass Court Stargazing Night."

Sam craned his neck and peered up. This rooftop deck was the perfect place to look at the stars.

"And guess what?" Mama Lyla said. "We asked the mayor if it would be possible to turn off the streetlights tonight so that we could see even more stars—and she said yes!"

"But we can see stars when the streetlights are on," Sam said, confused.

"Yeah," Sofia added. "I make a wish on a different star every night."

"True," Aunt Charlie said with a knowing smile. "But just wait until you see the night sky without all this light pollution interfering!"

"Will we actually see constellations?" Sofia asked.

"Yes!" Aunt Charlie replied. "The stars, the

Sun, and the Moon all create amazing sights in the sky for people around the world to enjoy."

With a big smile on her face, Mama Lyla perched on one of the lounge chairs.

"I'll never forget my trip to Alaska," she began.

Sofia knew from the warm sparkle in her mom's voice that they were about to hear a story. Sam and Sofia sat down, too.

Mama Lyla grabbed a nearby broom and mimicked paddling with it, as if the chair had turned into a kayak. "I put on my warmest clothes and went out on a giant lake. The northern lights lit up the dark sky, shimmering green and gold and purple. It was breathtaking."

"Wow," Sam breathed.

"I had a nighttime adventure like that, too—but it wasn't cold at all," Papai Luiz said. "I was on the walkway to the Garganta del Diablo—"

"The Devil's Throat?" Sofia gasped.

Papai Luiz smiled at her. "Yes, that's the English translation," he said. "It's a massive waterfall between Brazil and Argentina, where water flows in from three sides. I was on the path over the falls, with a full moon gleaming above me. That's when I saw it."

He spun and grabbed the broom from Mama Lyla, using the end to trace an arc through the air. "A moonbow!"

Sam pictured it in his mind. "Is that like a rainbow?" he asked.

"Yes, caused by the light of the moon," said Papai Luiz. "The spray from the waterfall refracted the moonbeams, making a band across the sky."

"People all around the world have been looking at the sky and the stars for years," Aunt Charlie said, "and without the help of the high-tech gadgets and gizmos we have today. In fact, the ancient Maya civilization inspired our star-gazing soirée this evening."

"Ancient Maya? They lived in Mexico, right?" Sam asked.

"Yes, some of them did," Aunt Charlie replied. "El Castillo is an ancient pyramid at Chichén Itzá in Mexico. It's also called the Temple of Kukulkan, named after a Maya deity believed to control the Sun."

"Kukulkan?" Sam asked.

Aunt Charlie nodded. "That's his name. According to stories, he takes the form of a feathered serpent. His pyramid holds many mysteries, and one of them is revealed twice a year during the equinox."

"Wait—what's an equinox?" Sofia spoke up.

"The equinox happens when the Sun crosses the equator," Aunt Charlie said. "It's when the day and the night are the same length. That's what made me think of El Castillo."

"Is something special going to happen there?" Sofia said.

Aunt Charlie nodded. She reached for some terra-cotta pots and started to stack them in a pyramid.

"Twice a year," she said, "during the equinox, the mysterious shadow of a serpent appears on the pyramid steps."

Her voice dropped to a hush as she took the broom from Papai Luiz and held it in front of the pots, casting a shadow.

"As the sun moves across the sky," she

continued, "the snake's shadow crawls down the side of the pyramid to connect with an enormous snake head carved in stone."

Sam and Sofia watched closely as Aunt Charlie's broom shadow moved down the pyramid of pots.

"By the time the Sun sets," Aunt Charlie continued, "you can see the full shape of the snake, clear as day."

In the silence that followed, Aunt Charlie smiled mysteriously. "And who can guess what today is?" she asked.

2

Star Charts

Sam felt excitement bubble inside him. "The equinox?" he guessed.

"That's right!" said Aunt Charlie. "Seemed like the perfect time to gaze up at the stars."

For a moment, all Sam could think about was

14

how badly he wanted to see the shadow snake slither along the side of El Castillo. When his eyes met Sofia's gaze, he could tell that she was thinking the same thing.

Aunt Charlie leaned over to rummage through her boxes. She pulled out several pairs of binoculars, pieces of her telescope, red-light flashlights, and—

"Oh, stars above!" Aunt Charlie exclaimed, making Sam and Sofia jump. "I can't believe I left the star charts back at my lab! Would you two mind getting them for me?"

"No, of course not," Sam said. Sofia was already on her feet, ready to go.

"You'll find them in the corner, by the shelves over the outlets," Aunt Charlie said. "No rush in bringing them back. We won't need them until nightfall. Thank you!"

And then, Sam couldn't be entirely sure, but he almost thought that Aunt Charlie winked.

Sam and Sofia didn't talk until they had made their way down from the deck, all the way through the community center, and were hurrying along the sidewalk to Sam's house.

"Are you thinking what I'm thinking?" Sam asked.

Sofia nodded. "We have to go, right?" she said in a quiet voice. "To see the snake shadow at El Castillo? It only happens twice a year—and it's going to happen *today!*"

"I don't want to miss it, either," Sam said.

Aunt Charlie's lab was in a converted garage attached to their house. After Compass Community Center, Sam and Sofia spent more time there than just about anywhere else. When Sam heard Aunt Charlie tinkering in the lab late at night, he always knew she had a new idea that was so exciting she couldn't sleep.

It wasn't so long ago that one of her new ideas had changed *everything*. The cherry-red scooter looked like an ordinary vehicle, with the addition of a high-tech touch screen. There was something about the way the scooter gleamed that had drawn both Sam and Sofia to it right away. Aunt Charlie had encouraged them to check out the scooter while she took a phone call. They sat on the seats, held onto the handles, and typed a destination onto the touch screen.

Neither one had expected the blazing globe of light that surrounded the scooter, or that with a **Whiz . . . Zoom . . . FOOP!** it would transport them around the world.

That first trip across the world was only the start of their unexpected, globetrotting adventures. Ever since, they kept the red scooter charged up and ready to go. Sam and Sofia never knew just where—or when—they'd need to go exploring.

They were always ready to go at a moment's notice, and a new moment had arrived.

As their eyes adjusted to the dimness of the lab, Sam let out an excited laugh.

"Look," he said, pointing at the tarp covering the red scooter. "Aunt Charlie left the star charts right on top." He carefully moved them to the counter, then paused before slipping the star charts into his messenger bag.

"Do you think she meant for us to travel to El Castillo all along?" Sofia asked. "Here I thought it was *our* idea."

"Well, you know what Aunt Charlie always says," Sam replied. "Great minds think alike!"

Sofia yanked the tarp off the scooter. They checked to make sure the battery was full, then climbed aboard.

Sam's finger brushed against the touch screen. It began to glow as the image of a globe appeared and began to spin in slow rotation.

HELLO EXPLORERS!

Where would you like to travel?

Sam's fingers went **tap-tap-tap** as he typed on the touchscreen:

EL CASTILLO, CHICHÉN ITZÁ, MEXICO

"Ready?" Sam asked Sofia.

"Ready!" she replied, her eyes twinkling. "*Vamos!*"

Sam took a deep breath and pushed the button. A bubble of light surrounded them, gold and glittering.

Whiz . . . Zoom . . . FOOP!

3

El Caracol

Sam knew they were no longer on Compass Court before he even opened his eyes. As he listened to the sounds around him, his brain churned with questions.

Where will we hide the red scooter?

Who will we meet?

How close can we get to the pyramid?

When Sam's vision came into focus, he saw that he and Sofia were in a shady grove of trees. Sofia had already jumped off the scooter.

"Come on, Sam!" she urged. "Let's find El Castillo!"

Once they made sure that the red scooter was hidden among the trees, Sam and Sofia dashed toward the sunlight streaming through the edge of the grove. The low hum Sam had heard before grew steadily louder until he realized it was dozens of different voices—maybe *hundreds* of different voices—all talking at once. It wasn't long before another thought struck him: The voices weren't speaking English.

Of course, Sam thought, grinning to himself. *We're in Mexico!*

"There are so many people here," Sofia said in a low voice as they stepped forward to see the crowd. "It's like a party!"

"I guess we're not the only ones who want to see the shadow snake," Sam said. "Can you tell which language they're speaking? Is it Spanish?"

Sofia was silent for a moment as she listened. "I think they're speaking a lot of different languages," she finally said. "Which makes sense—there are probably tourists here from all over the world. I know I heard a snippet of English . . . and a little bit of French . . ."

"*Oui, oui,*" Sam agreed, smiling as he remembered some of the French they'd learned.

"But mostly Spanish," Sofia continued. "It sounds a lot like Portuguese. Not enough that I can understand all of it . . . but every once in a while, I hear a word or phrase that sounds familiar."

They walked through a wide lawn, which was crowded with people sharing picnics and hanging out. Sam didn't pay much attention to all the people, though. He was focused on El Castillo. The pyramid was more impressive than Sam could have imagined.

The stony sides of El Castillo jutted up from the ground, an imposing structure against a bright blue sky that was dotted with puffy clouds. Each of the pyramid's four sides featured a stairway that led to the top.

Sofia shielded her eyes and glanced at the sky to find the position of the sun. "Uh-oh," she told Sam. "We were worried about missing the shadows, but I think we got here a little too early. It's not even midday, and the serpent shadow won't be fully visible until sundown."

"That means we have plenty of time to explore," Sam told her. "Look, that sign says there's an observatory over there. El Caracol. Let's check it out."

They walked along a dusty road for a few minutes.

"El Caracol," Sofia said thoughtfully. "That's funny. In Portuguese, *caracol* means 'snail.'"

"Snail?" Sam repeated.

Sofia nodded. "The last thing snails remind me of are stars," she said with a giggle. "Don't get me wrong, I like snails. They're really slimy and they make their very own houses, which is pretty incredible—"

"El Caracol," a man nearby said.

Both Sam and Sofia stopped short and turned to face the man. He was about the same age as

Aunt Charlie, with a few gray streaks in his shiny black hair. His face crinkled into a warm smile as he spoke.

Beside him was a cart that displayed brightly colored postcards and other small souvenirs.

"*Lo siento*, I did not mean to eavesdrop," he said, holding up his hands. "My name is Miguel. You reminded me of my niece, Amalia. She said the same thing when she first visited El Caracol. I thought you would be interested to know that in Spanish, caracol means 'snail,' but it also means 'seashell.' "

"So it *is* close to Portuguese," Sofia said thoughtfully. "But what does that have to do with an observatory?"

Miguel waved his arm in the direction of El Caracol. "It may be hard to imagine now, but long ago, El Caracol twisted up to the sky in a spiral. Just like a seashell or a snail's shell curves into a spiral."

Sam squinted up at the structure and pictured it in his mind. "I can see it," Sam said happily. He lifted his camera and began taking pictures.

Click-click! Click-click!

Sam had taken some great pictures from this angle, but he had a sudden and intense longing to go closer—and higher. He saw the ropes that kept people from climbing the crumbling stone steps, but he still wanted a better view.

Maybe Miguel could help.

"You said your niece visits you here," Sam said. "Are you the—the *curator*?" Sam wasn't sure it was the right word.

Miguel shook his head and gestured toward his cart. "No," he replied. "I'm a vendor. I sell postcards. Why? You look disappointed."

"No! I'm not. Not really, I mean," Sam said. "I was just hoping we could get a little closer. I'd love to take a better picture of that window."

"You and me both, *mi amigo*," Miguel replied. "But this is a protected site. So even if I could get past the barriers, I wouldn't do it. We must preserve El Caracol for future scientists and historians to study. And for all the people. It belongs to us now. There are visitors almost every day of the year. Of course, it gets especially busy around the equinox."

Sam and Sofia exchanged a glance. "That's what brought us here," Sam told Miguel.

"I had a feeling," Miguel said. "I might just have a postcard for you." As Miguel flipped through his display, Sam couldn't take his eyes off the postcards. There were photos of lush landscapes throughout Mexico . . . tropical jungles where bright birds perched in the trees . . . dusty deserts studded with spiky cacti . . . sleek cities with towering buildings made of glass and chrome . . . remote lagoons that almost seemed to glow under the starlit sky . . .

And then, Miguel found the postcard he was looking for: a close-up of El Caracol's crumbling dome, complete with a spiral staircase and a gaping window.

"*Aquí!*" Miguel announced as he plucked it from the display. "I know it's not the same as taking the photo yourself, but I want you to have it."

Sam looked up in surprise. "Really?" he asked. "Are you sure?"

"*Sí,*" Miguel replied, nodding. "Anyone who appreciates the wonder of El Caracol as you do deserves it."

Then he turned to Sofia. "Which one do you like the best?"

"They're all beautiful," she said. "Why are some of them photographs and some of them paintings?"

Miguel puffed up with pride. "Amalia painted those," he said.

"Really?" Sofia said. "She's good! I mean, she's *great!*"

Miguel beamed at her. "That's what I always say!" he replied. "She lives in Mexico City and paints almost every day. Every month, I get a parcel from her with more postcards to sell. And at the time of the equinox, I always sell out. No matter how many she sends, *los turistas* snap them right up!"

"Hibiscus," Sofia said, pointing at a postcard with a large pink flower on it. "Mrs. Necochea grows that in her garden at home in Compass Court."

"Here, we call it *hibisco*," Miguel said. "Amalia's favorite."

He held out the card. "Would you like it?"

"Thank you!" Sofia said. "It reminds me of home *and* Mexico!"

Just then, another postcard caught Sam's eye. This one was different from the others. It didn't have a colorful flower or a spiny cactus. Instead, it showed the night sky, with bright stars no bigger than pin pricks. As Sam looked at the card, he noticed that some of the stars were connected by a single golden thread. The thread almost formed the shape of an S.

And that gave him an idea.

"Is that a constellation?" Sam asked, pointing at the thread.

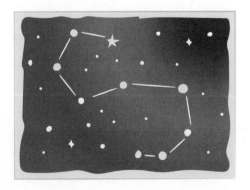

Miguel shrugged. "Only the artist knows," he replied. "I'd ask Amalia for you, but she can be hard to reach so far away in Mexico City. Most afternoons, she's painting somewhere at La Casa Azul."

"Would it be okay if I took a picture of this postcard?" Sam asked Miguel.

"I can do even better than that," Miguel replied. "Keep it."

Sam shook his head. "No—no, I can't," he replied. "It's too beautiful. Besides, it's the equinox! You need every postcard to sell."

Miguel's whole face crinkled up as he smiled at Sam and Sofia. "Art is meant to be shared, not just sold," he told them. "I want you to have it."

A chattering crowd of tourists appeared over the ridge, approaching the stony steps of El Caracol. Miguel began to straighten his postcard display.

"Customers!" he said brightly to Sam and

Sofia. "If this is anything like the last equinox, I'll be sold out by sundown."

"Let's get out of the way," Sam told Sofia in a low voice. Then, louder, he said, "Thank you, Miguel!"

"Thank you for *everything*," Sofia added.

They were quiet as they walked back toward the pyramid at El Castillo.

"This way," Sam said, nudging Sofia back toward the grove of trees. "That's where we hid the red scooter."

"But we can't go back to Compass Court yet," Sofia said. "The sun is still high in the sky."

"Who said anything about going back to Compass Court?" Sam asked with a smile.

"What are you thinking?" Sofia asked, her eyes bright with excitement.

4

The Mysterious Constellation

"Let's go to Mexico City!" Sam announced.

"Mexico City!" Sofia exclaimed. "To meet Amalia?"

"We can get any extra postcards she has and

bring them back for Miguel to sell," Sam said. "It's the least we could do. He gave us these for free!"

"I like the way you think," Sofia said.

"And we can ask Amalia about this postcard, too," Sam continued. "Look at the golden thread. What do you see?"

"A squiggle . . . a letter S . . . a snake?" Sofia guessed.

"Yes!" Sam said. "Let's see if we can find it on Aunt Charlie's star chart!"

Sam pulled the star chart out of his messenger bag. He and Sofia compared the chart and the card in silence, but couldn't find a constellation on the chart that matched the postcard.

"Do you think," Sam said, "it could be a constellation of Kukulkan?"

"Kukulkan?" Sofia asked. "Why does that name sound familiar?"

"El Castillo is also called . . ." Sam hinted.

"The temple of Kukulkan!" Sofia said. "Kukulkan is the snake god from the Maya stories Aunt Charlie told us about."

"Exactly," Sam said. "What if Amalia found out about a Kukulkan constellation, and painted it? When we get home, we could tell Aunt Charlie all about it," Sam began. Then a new idea made his face light up. "Maybe we could even show her! Tonight, during the star party on the deck!"

"To Mexico City!" Sofia cried. "*Vamos!*"

Sam and Sofia climbed aboard the red scooter. "Do you remember where Miguel said Amalia paints in the afternoon?" Sam asked.

Sofia nodded vigorously. "I do!" she said. "La Casa Azul. Which means 'The Blue House' in Portuguese."

"The Blue House," Sam repeated. "Well, hopefully that means it will be easy to find."

"Here's how you spell it," Sofia said. As she told him each letter, Sam tapped on the touchscreen.

Whiz . . . Zoom . . . FOOP!

5

La Casa Azul

The red scooter brought Sam and Sofia to a small alleyway dotted with flowers in Mexico City. As soon as the flashing lights dimmed, they could hear the traffic rushing through the nearby streets.

"See any blue houses?" Sam asked Sofia.

She shook her head. "Not yet," she told him.

But they didn't have to explore far. As soon as they left the alley, they saw it: a bright blue wall.

No—not just a wall. It was an entire blue building! That wasn't the only color, though. Red trim and a green door made the building look cheerful and inviting. Sam raised his camera to frame the photo.

Click-click!

"Check out that sign," Sofia said, pointing at big, bold letters over the door. "MUSEO FRIDA KAHLO. Hmm . . . in Portuguese, *museu* means 'museum.' "

"Frida Kahlo! I know her!" Sam exclaimed. "I

mean, I don't *know* her, but I know who she is. She's a really famous Mexican artist."

"This must be a museum of her artwork," Sofia replied. "Why did the scooter bring us to a museum? Amalia paints at a blue house."

Sam was confused, too. "At least it's blue," he said. "Amalia is an artist, too. Maybe we'll find her in the museum."

"There's only one way to find out," Sofia said.

"Let's go!" Sam said.

"*Vamos!*" Sofia echoed.

Inside the museum, there were so many incredible things to see that for a few moments, Sam and Sofia forgot the reason they were there: to look for Amalia.

"There's a kitchen? In the museum?" Sam said in confusion.

"Sam," Sofia began, "I don't think this is just a museum. I think this is where Frida Kahlo actually lived!"

"Are you serious?" Sam asked.

Sofia nodded eagerly. "Check it out—there's

a dining room, and a living room, and even bedrooms," she explained, showing him a map of Museo Frida Kahlo. And if it was her house *before* it was a museum, the name makes sense. La Casa Azul!"

"Maybe Aunt Charlie and I should paint our house blue," Sam said.

"Only if you let me help," Sofia replied. "Let's get a closer look at the kitchen." It was such a cheerful room, with a bright yellow floor, yellow and blue tiles, and handmade pots and spoons.

Sofia stood next to a large bowl and pretended to stir something inside it. "I'm making tortillas!" she told Sam. "Just like Mama taught me."

Sam grinned as he held up his camera. "Say cheese!" he told her.

Sofia started to reply, but then a funny smile crossed her face. "*Queso!*" she said as she posed, answering him in Spanish instead.

After they toured the kitchen, Sam and Sofia

moved into the living room.

"Sam, check it out!" she exclaimed. "Frida Kahlo actually painted these paintings. Painted them with her own hands! They're her own original artwork!"

"That's her," Sam said, pointing at a painting of a beautiful woman surrounded by plants and animals. There was a small sign beneath it that read *FRIDA KAHLO*.

"Ooh, is it a self-portrait?" Sofia asked eagerly. Then she noticed another painting across the room. "Look—Frida Kahlo is in that painting, too! And that one!"

With her dark hair, heavy eyebrows, and colorful clothing, the artist was unmistakable in each painting.

"I wonder why Frida Kahlo painted so many self-portraits," Sofia said.

Sam, deep in thought, crossed the room to glance out the window at one of the courtyards. "I don't know—" he started to say.

But something he saw outside caused his words to trail off unexpectedly. Sam lifted his camera to his eye, zoomed in a little, and made sure the shot was in focus.

Click-click!

Right after he took the picture, Sam examined it on the screen on the back of his camera. "Sofia?" he called.

"What's up?" she asked from across the room, where she was studying a sculpture.

"Can you come over and look at this?" Sam asked her.

"Sure." Sofia crossed the room to meet him.

When Sam held out his camera, she looked at the picture.

"It's a girl in a courtyard," Sofia said, "with some big plants around her." She glanced up. "Is this here?"

Sam nodded. "I took it just now. This—" he paused for a moment to zoom in on the  picture again— "is the important thing. Look at the flower in her hair."

As Sofia gazed at the screen, her eyes went wide. She would've recognized that flower anywhere.

"It's a hibiscus flower!" she said. "Just like the one on Amalia's postcard."

"Now look at *that*," Sam said, moving the image on the screen.

"She has a sketchbook!" Sofia cried. "Is that who I think it is?"

6

The Girl in the Courtyard

Sam and Sofia hurried outside, where large, leafy plants created cool clusters of shade. The airy courtyard even had a large reflecting pool filled with clear water.

As they approached the girl with the flower in her hair, Sam cleared his throat. "Excuse me," he said. "Are you . . . Amalia?"

The girl looked up in surprise. "*Sí*," she replied, nodding her head. "Who are you?"

Sam and Sofia quickly introduced themselves.

"We met your uncle at El Caracol," Sofia said. "He showed us your postcards—you're so talented! That's how we recognized you, actually. From the hibiscus in your hair. He told us you like to draw at La Casa Azul."

Amalia's face brightened. "Are you fans of Frida Kahlo's work, too?" she asked. "She's my favorite artist!"

"We saw some of her self-portraits," Sam replied. He reached into his pocket to grab the starry postcard. "I wanted to ask you—"

But Amalia was caught up with excitement and kept talking about Frida Kahlo. "Did you tour her studio?" she asked. "*Ay!* It's magical just to stand there and imagine her painting, breathing the same air . . ."

"Her studio?" Sam repeated. "No, I don't think we saw that. We went to the kitchen, the dining room, the living room . . ."

Amalia jumped up from the bench and stuffed her sketchbook into her backpack. "Come with me," she announced. "I know you'll love it!"

Frida Kahlo's art studio was more fascinating than Sam could have ever anticipated. Sunlight streamed through dozens of windows, offering lots of bright light for any type of artwork.

"Wow," Sam breathed. "Her actual easel!"

"And her paints!" Sofia added. "Too bad, it looks like they're all dried up."

Sam took a closer look at the tiny bottles of powder in brilliant shades of red, yellow, green, orange, blue, and purple. "You know what?" he said. "I think these are supposed to be powder."

"*Sí*," Amalia said, nodding. "They are

50

pigments. She would have added water or oil or some other liquid to turn them into paint."

"Look—these are her paintbrushes!" Sofia exclaimed.

"And look over here," Sam said as he walked around the easel. "It's her wheelchair."

"I didn't know Frida Kahlo used a wheelchair," Sofia said.

"Señora Frida had a lot of health problems," Amalia said. "She had a really bad disease called polio when she was a little girl, and then, when she was older, she was in a serious bus accident and never recovered all the way. That's actually why she became a painter instead of a doctor. She had to spend so much time in bed that she started painting to pass the time."

"You mean she painted in that bed? Right over there?" Sofia asked, pointing to a room next to the art studio.

"I want to show you something," Amalia said.

Sam and Sofia followed her to Frida Kahlo's bed. On the ceiling above it was a mirror. The friends had to twist their necks to look up at its shiny surface.

"Frida had a mirror put on the ceiling so she could see herself to paint her self-portraits," Amalia explained. "Her paintings were like nothing that had ever been created before. With them, she captured the spirit of Mexico—and her own fierce and determined spirit."

Sam and Sofia listened quietly.

"My mom loves Frida's work," Amalia said. "She taught me all about her growing up. She's inspired people for generations. Can you imagine being the kind of artist whose artwork changes the world?" She looked up at the mirror. "I hope that someday I can be like that."

Sam wanted to remember this special moment forever. He held up his camera. "Hey, can we all take a selfie?" he asked. "So we can

tell everyone we knew you before you became a super-famous artist?"

A smile crossed Amalia's face. "Sure," she replied. "Let's take our picture by Frida's easel."

The three friends crowded together. Sam held out his camera. "Say—" he began.

Before he could finish, a security guard marched up to them.

"*Perdóname*," she said, frowning. "Do you have a photography permit?"

7

Busted!

Sam swallowed hard as he lowered his camera. "A—a what?" he asked in a quivering voice.

"A photography permit," the guard repeated. "You're not allowed to take photos in here without purchasing a special permit. Where is your ticket?"

Busted, Sam thought. He looked over at Sofia, hoping she had an idea for how to get them out of this jam. But Sofia looked as stunned as Sam felt.

Then, to their surprise, Amalia laughed. "Rosa, they're with me!" she said in a cheerful voice.

The guard's frown softened. "Rules are rules, Amalia," she said.

"I have a membership to the museum, don't I, Rosa?" Amalia asked. "Don't I visit almost every day?"

"*Sí*," the guard admitted. Then a slow smile crossed her face. Sam could tell right away that Rosa and Amalia were pals, which made his worry melt away.

"*Mis amigos* and I were about to leave, anyway," Amalia said, wiggling her fingers in a little wave. "But I will probably see you tomorrow."

"See you later, then," Rosa said, nodding her head. "But don't forget! No photos without a permit."

Sam held his breath until the three friends were standing on the sidewalk outside the museum. When he went to exhale at last, he found himself laughing in relief.

"Thank you so much," he said to Amalia. "I didn't know I needed a permit to take pictures. I take pictures all the time, everywhere I go! You really saved me."

"*De nada*," Amalia said, laughing with him. "Everyone here knows me. Some guards are stricter than others. I'm sorry Rosa gave you a hard time."

"It's okay," Sam said. "There was actually another reason we wanted to meet you."

"Oh?" Amalia asked.

"Your uncle told us that he always sells out of postcards on the day of the equinox," Sofia explained. "So we thought if you have any extra cards we could bring them back to him."

"I'm almost done with a whole new set," Amalia said. "But there's no way to get them to Tío Miguel today. El Caracol is seventeen hours away."

Sam and Sofia smiled at each other. "Let's just say we have a quicker way to get there," Sam said. "Follow us!"

At the red scooter, Sofia turned to Amalia with her eyes twinkling. "Can you keep a secret?" she asked.

Amalia nodded.

Her mouth formed the shape of a perfect O as Sam and Sofia took turns telling her that their shiny red scooter was no ordinary ride.

"You just type a location on the screen—any location—and it takes you there?" Amalia asked in disbelief.

"That's right," Sofia replied.

Amalia clapped her hands in delight. "What a wonderful story!" she said. "I will tell Tío Miguel that my new friends have amazing imaginations, just like Frida Kahlo!"

Sam couldn't blame Amalia for her response. He didn't know if he would believe what the scooter could do if he hadn't experienced it for himself.

"Trust us," he said. "We can definitely get the paintings to your uncle in time for him to sell them today."

"Even if that's true," Amalia began, "there's just one problem. My postcards are not quite finished yet. But . . . maybe you could help me finish them."

"Absolutely!" Sofia replied. "I mean, I'd love to help if I can. Sam's the artist, though."

"Don't worry, I'll show you exactly what to do," Amalia promised.

"Let's do it!" Sam said eagerly.

"Okay," Sofia agreed as a grin spread across her face. "I'll help however I can."

"We can take the metrobus to one of my other favorite painting spots in Mexico City," Amalia continued, growing more excited with every word. "El Jardín Botánico de UNAM!"

Sam and Sofia exchanged a glance. They weren't sure what that was.

"Wait a second—I think I can figure it out!" Sofia said. "Jardín Botánico in Spanish sounds a lot like *jardim botânico* in Portuguese, which means, in English, 'botanical garden'! I don't know about 'de UNAM,' though."

Amalia clapped her hands in delight. "You got it!" she said. "UNAM means the Universidad Nacional Autónoma de México. It's one of the best universities in the world. Come on. There's a metrobus stop near here. Hopefully we won't have to wait very long—"

"Or we could take the red scooter, and we wouldn't have to wait at all," Sam spoke up. "Want to try it? You could sit in the front and type on the touchscreen."

"Sure," Amalia said. "I can drive a scooter."

Sam and Sofia smiled at each other. Sam suspected that Amalia was humoring them, but soon enough she'd see just what the scooter could do.

As the friends climbed aboard the red scooter, the spinning globe appeared on the screen.

"*Increíble*," Amalia whispered.

"Don't forget to hold on tight!" Sam reminded her.

"I will," Amalia promised. Her fingers moved quickly as she typed:

El Jardín Botánico de UNAM,
Mexico City, Mexico

Whiz . . . Zoom . . . FOOP!

8

The Hidden Pond

Moments later, the red scooter arrived near el Jardín Botánico.

"We're—we're here!" Amalia gasped. "You said we would—and I didn't think—but we did—I . . . I can't believe it!"

"Pretty amazing, isn't it?" Sofia asked, grinning.

"How does it work?" Amalia marveled. She walked around the scooter in a state of amazement, admiring it from every angle.

"We don't know exactly how," Sam said, his palms in the air. "I haven't figured out a way to ask Aunt Charlie yet."

"You could travel the whole world!" Amalia said.

Sam and Sofia exchanged a smile. That was exactly what they hoped to do.

Then Sam sniffed the air. "Mmm," he said. "Something smells delicious!"

"It's Abuela's tamales," Amalia explained, pointing to a food cart near the entrance. "She's not my *abuela*—that's Spanish for *grandmother*—but everybody calls her that. Her tamales are the best in the city! Want to share some?"

"You bet!" Sofia said, licking her lips. "I loooooove tamales!"

"Good," Amalia said. "I could use something in my stomach after that ride."

"What's a tamale?" Sam asked.

"You've never had one?" Amalia asked. "This is your lucky day!"

Sam and Sofia parked the scooter behind some tall cacti before they followed Amalia over to the food cart. After Amalia ordered in rapid-fire Spanish, Abuela nodded and smiled.

She lifted the lid off a big steel pot, releasing clouds of billowing steam into the air. Then, with a pair of long-handled tongs, she carefully plucked three tamales out of the pot.

"*Para ti*," she said happily. "For you."

"*Gracias,*" Amalia said.

"*Gracias,*" Sam and Sofia repeated.

Sam studied his tamale carefully. He wasn't quite sure how to eat it, so he was grateful when Amalia showed him exactly what to do.

"See this?" she asked, touching the papery wrapping. "This is the corn husk. We *don't* eat that part."

"I love how tamales are made," Sofia said. "They're all wrapped up, like a present!"

"Here. Pull apart the corn husk, like this." Amalia demonstrated for Sam. "Now eat!"

Sam stared at the steaming pocket of dough in his hand. "What's inside?" he asked.

"Take a bite and find out," Sofia said, before chomping into her own.

Amalia smiled as she handed Sam a fork.

"The dough we call *masa*. It's made from . . . uh . . . you would call it corn flour, I think."

"That's right," Sofia said as she took another huge bite.

"And inside, well, there are lots of different types of tamales, but these have chicken and mole sauce," Amalia continued.

"This mole sauce is soooo good," Sofia said. "Spicy and smoky and a tiny bit sweet."

"That's because it has a little chocolate in it," Amalia said.

All the talking about the tamales had made Sam even hungrier. He scooped up a big bite of his tamale and popped it in his mouth.

"Wow," Sam mumbled through a mouthful of tamale. "Wow!"

The tamale tasted even better than it smelled. The *masa* dough was soft and flavorful, the chicken was tender and juicy, and the deep flavors of the reddish-brown mole sauce were unlike anything Sam had ever eaten before.

Sam swallowed his bite and grinned at Amalia. "If I lived here, I would eat tamales every day," he told her.

"Believe me, it's tempting!" Amalia replied.

After they finished the tamales, Amalia led them into el Jardín Botánico. Stepping through the gates was like entering a mysterious world filled with rare and incredible plants.

"El Jardín Botánico only has plants that are native to Mexico," Amalia explained. "The garden was founded to preserve and protect our special plants, and to study them so we could learn all about them. There's a garden for plants with healing powers and so many cacti you wouldn't even believe it."

"How many?" Sofia asked curiously.

"I think there are about eight hundred different kinds in Mexico!" Amalia told her.

"Yowch! Don't get too close," Sofia joked.

"They aren't just prickly, though," Amalia told her. "Some cacti have beautiful flowers. Some are edible. There's even one type of cactus that can be used as a source of water in the driest desert!"

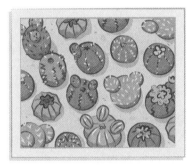

She led Sam and Sofia over a twisty path to an area of the botanical garden with taller, leafier trees that cast shadows across the landscape. Sam tilted his head. He could hear the sound of water cascading over rocks.

"Here it is!" Amalia said proudly. "The hidden water lily pond."

The pond was so beautiful that Sam couldn't

say a word. He was too busy photographing it.
He didn't want to forget a single detail.

Click-click! Click-click!

Amalia opened her backpack and pulled
out a stack of painted postcards and three ink
pens. "The painting part is already done," she
explained to Sam and Sofia. "But I need help
adding lines for definition."

Amalia passed out the ink
pens. Then she showed Sam
and Sofia how to find the
faint pencil marks she had
sketched on each postcard
and add a little bit of ink to
make each element of her
paintings more distinct.

"This pen is so cool!" Sam said as he tried it
out.

"Keep it," Amalia told him. When Sam started
to protest, she insisted. "You can take it home

and make your own artwork with it."

"Thank you," Sam said gratefully.

While the three friends chatted and added ink to Amalia's paintings, no one noticed the time passing, or the long shadows creeping across the pond.

Suddenly, Sam jumped back. "What is that?" he shouted as a snake slithered past them. It was a bright shade of reddish-orange, mottled with black and cream bands.

"That's just a little milk snake. It's harmless," Amalia replied.

Click-click!

Sam took a quick photo of the milk snake as it slithered away.

"With so many plants that are protected here,

there are a lot of amazing animals and insects, too," Amalia was saying. "We do need to watch out for rattlesnakes and tarantulas, though."

"Rattlesnakes *and* tarantulas?" Sofia asked. "Wow! I've never seen them in the wild before!"

"If we do, I'll get a picture," Sam told her. "But I don't want to get any closer than that!"

"Don't worry," Amalia assured him. "I've never seen either one here at my favorite painting spot."

Sam put the cap on his ink pen and looked at his photo of the milk snake. The snake!

Suddenly, Sam remembered the whole reason for their trip to Mexico. He glanced around the pond in alarm as he realized the light had shifted, bathing the area in the warm glow of sunset.

"Sofia!" he said, jumping up. "El Castillo!"

They'd have to hurry to get back to El Castillo before they missed the appearance of the shadow snake.

"Will we make it back in time?" Sofia asked.

9

Sunset

"I didn't realize it was getting so late," Sam told Amalia. "We'd better get back to El Castillo."

"Of course!" she said. "The sun is starting to set. You don't want to miss the shadow serpent's appearance."

"Come with us!" Sam urged. "You can give the postcards to your uncle!"

"Did you tell him about the scooter?" Amalia asked.

Sam looked at Sofia. "No," he said. "You're the only person we've told here in Mexico."

Amalia shook her head and thought for a long moment. "I don't know how we'd explain to him how I got there," she finally said. "And my parents would get worried. I'm supposed to be home soon."

"You're probably right," Sam said.

"We understand," Sofia said.

"Well, can we at least take you back to La Casa Azul first?" Sofia said.

"Don't worry about me," Amalia told her. "I can always take the metrobus. You two have to hurry! *¡Rapido!* There isn't a moment to lose! I can't believe I almost forgot about the equinox!"

"I almost forgot something, too," Sam said. He pulled the constellation postcard out of her pocket. "Your uncle—your *tío*—gave me this."

A wide smile spread across Amalia's face. "Ahhh! I remember when I painted it!" she said.

"I wanted to ask you about this constellation," Sam said, tapping the sky. "It's not on any star chart I've seen. Is it . . . could it be a constellation of Kukulkan?"

"The snake god?" Amalia asked in surprise. She took the painting from Sam, tilted it to a new angle, and slowly nodded.

"You know a lot about El Castillo," she said. "I've always loved the thought of Maya people long ago watching and studying the stars. So I painted real stars, in their real positions, and I connected them to form a new constellation."

She smiled. "I was thinking of Kukulkan when I painted it, but it's my own creation."

"I see," Sam said. He wasn't disappointed at all. In fact, he liked the constellation even more knowing Amalia had created it herself.

"So I was right!" he said with a smile.

"Well, it's not a *real* constellation," Amalia said.

"But all constellations are thought up by someone," Sam said.

"That's true," Amalia said, smiling back. "They're stories we tell each other."

"Maybe this constellation wasn't created by the Maya," Sofia added, "but they looked at the same stars."

The three of them looked up at the sky.

"Much has been forgotten or lost to time," said Amalia, "but we can still remember the old stories we *do* know . . . and dream up new ones, too."

"I like that," Sam said. "New stories for new adventures."

"And new friends," Sofia added.

After they exchanged addresses, Sam held up his camera. "We never did get that picture together," he said.

"Well, there are no guards to stop us here!" Amalia joked.

The three friends squeezed together as Sam held out the camera. "On the count of three, say . . ."

"Not cheese," Sofia said with a giggle. "How about . . . Frida?"

"Frida!" everyone said, smiling their best portrait smiles.

"I'm so glad I met you," Amalia told Sam and Sofia. "Please use the scooter to come back and visit me again! *¡Adios!*"

"*¡Adios!*" Sam and Sofia told her, saying goodbye in Spanish. Then, with one last look at the waterfall cascading over the lava rocks, they took off running down the twisty path toward the entrance to el Jardín Botánico.

Nestled behind the prickly cacti, the red scooter glittered in the light of the setting sun.

"I hope we're not too late," Sam said as they jumped onto the scooter. He started typing on the touch screen.

Whiz . . . Zoom . . . FOOP!

10

The Shadow Snake

When they returned to El Castillo, the crowds had swelled even larger. But even from a distance, Sam and Sofia could tell that the ancient pyramid was still bathed in golden sunlight. They weren't too late. They hadn't missed the shadow serpent's mysterious descent!

Sam stood still as he took it all in: the crowds, the pyramid, the sun slipping lower in the sky. But Sofia was already on the move.

"Come on," she called over her shoulder. "Let's find Miguel!"

They retraced their steps on the route to El Caracol and found Miguel right where they'd last seen him. Even though many more people were milling around, Miguel was already packing up his empty cart.

Sam knew what that meant. He and Sofia exchanged a glance and started to run toward him.

"Miguel!" Sofia called out as they approached.

Miguel looked up. His face broke into a wide smile. "*Mis amigos!*" he exclaimed. "What are you doing here? It's about time for Kukulkan to appear!"

"Special delivery!" Sam said. He thrust the parcel of postcards at Miguel.

Sam and Sofia only hesitated for a moment— just long enough to see the expression on Miguel's face change from one of confusion to amazement as he recognized that the postcards were from his niece. "But—what—how—" he stammered.

"*¡Adios!*" Sam and Sofia called out as they waved goodbye to Miguel one last time. Then they ran as fast as they could, dodging and weaving through the crowd until they were giggling too hard to take another step.

"He was so surprised!" Sam said.

"*And* he was sold out before sunset, just like he predicted," Sofia said happily. "Now he has plenty of postcards to sell to everybody visiting El Castillo."

"Speaking of El Castillo," Sam began, "let's try to get a little closer." He had a pretty good camera, but it wasn't powerful enough to get a photo of the shadow snake from so far away.

Sam and Sofia made their way as close to the front as they could. Everyone, who had been chatting and laughing before, was now quiet. A hush had fallen over the crowd as they stood together, bonded by the unforgettable event.

"Sam!" Sofia suddenly whispered. She pointed at the pyramid. "I see it!"

Sam saw it, too. It was so breathtaking that, at first, he didn't even think to take a picture. One of the pyramid's corners cast seven triangular shadows onto the side of the giant staircase. The shapes joined together to outline the bottom of a giant serpent's body, which ran the entire length of the pyramid, connecting to a stone snake head at the bottom.

Kukulkan, Sam thought in amazement. He lifted his camera to his face.

Click-click!

One shot. One perfect photo to remember an unbelievable phenomenon.

For several long minutes, Sam and Sofia stood together, part of the rapt and respectful crowd. It was an experience they would never forget.

As the sun continued to dip lower in the sky, though, the shadows grew longer, until they began to blend together. After a while, it wasn't

Whiz ... Zoom ... Foop!

as easy to see the mystical snake on the side of El Castillo.

And that, Sam and Sofia knew, meant it was time to go home.

They walked in silence back to the red scooter. It was waiting for them, right where they had left it.

Whiz . . . Zoom . . . Foop!

11

Star Party

Just like that, Sam and Sofia found themselves back in Aunt Charlie's lab. There was enough sun streaming through the windows that they could quickly plug in the red scooter, cover it with the tarp, and leave the lab—with the star charts Aunt Charlie had sent them to get, of course.

"The sun is almost down," Sofia said as they started walking back to Compass Community Center. "But the streetlights are flickering on, like they do every night."

"That's strange," Sam replied. "I hope the city didn't forget about our special stargazing party tonight."

"Me, too," Sofia said.

Up on the deck, the stargazing party was in full swing. All their friends and neighbors were there. Papai Luiz was helping Mikey and Ellie from the Compass Court Science Club make circular sky maps called planispheres. Meanwhile, Aunt Charlie was demonstrating how to use her telescope to their friends Ruby and Mani. Mama Lyla stood at the food table, which was brimming with space-themed snacks from moon cakes to starfruit.

Sofia turned to Sam with a beaming smile. "Let's join the star party!" she announced.

"Definitely," Sam agreed. "I just have to do one thing."

While Sofia started making a planisphere, Sam hurried across the deck to Aunt Charlie.

"There you are!" she said, her eyes twinkling like she knew a secret. "I haven't seen you and Sofia in a while."

"We wouldn't miss the star party for anything," Sam replied as he handed the star charts to Aunt Charlie. "They were on the scooter."

"Oh, were they?" Aunt Charlie said lightly.

Then she gave him a big wink.

"Aunt Charlie," Sam began, "It's getting pretty dark . . . but all the streetlights are still on."

Aunt Charlie put her arm around Sam's shoulders and gave him a squeeze. "Don't worry about the light pollution," she said. "If there's any problem with turning out the streetlights,

Mayor Arain is right over there, and she'll sort it out."

"The mayor came?" Sam asked in surprise.

"Of course! She loved the idea," Aunt Charlie said, glancing at her watch. "Anyway, if I'm not mistaken, the lights will go out right . . . about . . . now!"

As if on cue, every single streetlight suddenly went out, plunging Compass Court into darkness. Shrieks of glee and surprise echoed across the deck.

"It's time to use the red-light flashlights," Aunt Charlie announced. "They won't interfere with our ability to see celestial bodies."

As the chatter died down, a familiar hush fell over the crowd. It was the same kind of quiet that Sam and Sofia had heard at El Castillo.

Sofia was using a red-light flashlight to study her planisphere. The light lit up her face as she glanced over at Sam and smiled.

"Come on," she said in a low voice. "Let's see what we can find in the night sky."

Sam and Sofia sat down on a patchwork quilt and stared up into the darkness. At first, all Sam could see was the usual stuff: the Moon, the North Star, a smattering of smaller stars around the edges.

Then, as his eyes began to adjust to the darkness, Sam started to notice so much more. Tiny pinpricks of light were appearing all over the sky.

He pulled out the constellation postcard that Amalia had painted and studied it closely. There were stars on the postcard that he could find overhead!

Sam grabbed the ink pen Amalia had given him and used it to connect some of the stars, inventing his own new constellations.

"See that area that looks like a lit-up cloud?" Sofia whispered.

"I do," Sam replied.

"It's a nebula," Sofia told him. "New stars are being created there, and their light won't reach Earth for millions of years."

"Wow," Sam breathed.

He leaned back on his elbows and stared at the night sky in awe. Those stars shining down on him had shone down on the Maya people who had constructed El Castillo and El Caracol so many thousands of years before. They were connected by the starlight, across time and space.

He glanced around the deck, where the glow of the flashlights almost seemed to mirror the stars gleaming in the sky.

There was Papai Luiz and Mama Lyla, their heads close together as though they were sharing a secret. And there was Aunt Charlie, peering through her telescope. Mayor Arain, looking through some binoculars. Ellie and

Ruby ... Mani and Mikey, and even Mikey's dog, Scout ... all of them staring at the night sky, searching for whatever wonders would appear in the dark.

Sam smiled to himself.

Then he looked up too.

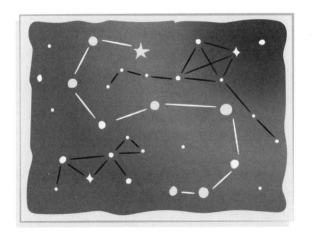

Spanish Terms

- **Abuela** - grandmother

- **El Castillo** - The Castle

- **El Caracol** - The Snail; The Seashell

- **Estrella** - Star   - **Hibisco** - Hibiscus

- **Increíble** - Incredible

- **Jardín botánico** - Botanical garden

- **La Casa Azul** - The Blue House

- **Los turistas** - The tourists

- **Mi(s) amigo(s)** - My friend(s)

- **Museo** - Museum   - **Queso** - Cheese

- **Sí** - Yes   - **Señora** - Ma'am   - **Tío** - Uncle

- **Universidad Nacional Autónoma de México** -
National Autonomous University of Mexico

Spanish Phrases

– **Adios** – Goodbye   – **¡Aquí!** – Here!

– **De nada** – You're welcome

– **Gracias** – Thank you   – **Hola** – Hello

– **Lo siento** – I'm sorry   – **Para ti** – For you

– **Perdóname** – Pardon me

– **¡Rapido!** – Quickly!

Portuguese Terms & Phrases

– **El Garganta del Diablo** – The Devil's Throat

– **El Caracol** – The Snail   – **Museu** – Museum

– **Jardim botânico** – Botanical garden

– **Vamos!** – Let's go!

Sofia and Sam's Snippets

The Mexican flag has three stripes: one green, one white, and one red. In the center is an image of an eagle with a snake in its mouth perched on a cactus.

An ancient Aztec legend tells the story of a new city formed where an eagle was seen eating a serpent on top of a cactus. According to the legend, that is how Mexico City was founded!

The Mexican flag

Ancient Maya and Aztec peoples were the first to grow and harvest cacao beans to make chocolate. Today, chocolate is still an important part of Mexican cuisine, used in savory mole sauce and a sweet, spiced version of hot chocolate called **champurrado**.

Corn, one of the most popular crops in the world, was cultivated more than 10,000 years ago by indigenous people in Mexico.

Frida Kahlo was born in Mexico City on July 6, 1907. However, she often told people her birthday was on July 7, 1910, which was the start of the Mexican Revolution. She wanted to share her birthday with her country!

Frida Kahlo endured many health problems throughout her life, but she didn't let them stop her from doing what she loved: painting. She remains one of Mexico's most important artists.

Some of Mexico's beaches glow in the dark! Bioluminescent waters filled with tiny plankton called **noctiluca scintillans** glitter with light when the plankton sense movement. On a dark night, the ocean waters sparkle and gleam like a starry sky.

Monarch butterflies migrate from Canada to Mexico every year. It can take four or five generations of butterflies to make the journey of over 2,500 miles.

Mariachi is a popular type of music in Mexico that dates back more than 200 years. **Mariachi** bands use trumpets and stringed instruments, like guitars and violins.

Dia de los Muertos, or Day of the Dead, is a holiday in Mexico that honors the memory of family ancestors. In their homes, families make special altars, called **ofrendas**, which are decorated with photos, candles, flowers, and favorite foods. Brightly colored sugar skulls are a famous part of **Dia de los Muertos**. They remind families to celebrate life and remember those who have passed.

Thousands of years ago, before the invention of high-tech instruments, the Maya studied the skies and made precise observations. They charted the movement of the Sun, the planets, and the stars, built observatories like El Caracol, and created a very accurate calendar.

Watercolor Postcard Craft

Materials:

- [ ] Watercolor paper cut to 4" by 6"
- [ ] Crayons (preferably light colors)
- [ ] Watercolor paint and paintbrush
- [ ] Ink pen (optional)

Amalia has a special technique for creating space scenes on some of her postcards.

Crayons are made of colored wax. When you draw with them, you transfer tiny bits of wax to the paper. Wax repels water, so when you add watercolor paint to your postcard, it won't stick to your crayon drawings.

Use this method inspired by Amalia to create a starry night scene on your postcard.